THE GOLDEN COMPASS

THE GRAPHIC NOVEL

PHILIP PULLMAN

THE GOLDEN COMPASS
THE GRAPHIC NOVEL

Adapted by Stéphane Melchior, art by Clément Oubrerie
Coloring by Clément Oubrerie with Philippe Bruno
Translated by Annie Eaton

ALFRED A. KNOPF NEW YORK

THIS IS A BORZOI BOOK PUBLISHED BY ALFRED A. KNOPF

Visit us on the Web! randomhousekids.com

Educators and librarians, for a variety of teaching tools, visit us at RHTeachersLibrarians.com

Library of Congress Cataloging-in-Publication Data is available upon request.
ISBN 978-0-553-53516-7 (trade) — ISBN 978-0-553-53517-4 (pbk.) —
ISBN 978-0-553-53518-1 (lib. bdg.) — ISBN 978-0-553-53519-8 (ebook)

MANUFACTURED IN CHINA
10 9 8 7 6 5

PART I

OXFORD

As you know, I set out for the North on a diplomatic mission to the king of Lapland. At least that's the reason I gave for the visit.

In fact, my real aim was to go farther north, right onto the ice, to discover what had happened to the Grumman expedition.

The devil! He knew about the wine, I'm sure of it.

Then we'll have to find another way.

You'll recognize Professor Stanislaus Grumman, of course.

That photogram was taken with a standard silver nitrate emulsion.

Here you see it developed with a new, specially prepared emulsion.

That light beside Grumman. Is it going up or coming down?

It's coming down, but it isn't light ...

... it's DUST.

Lord Asriel, you can't be serious?

Dust ... oh!

It can't be....

But how ...

It's heresy!

None of that nonsense. Roger is my nephew. He's Mr. Parslow's nephew too. I bet you didn't know that, 'cause I bet you never asked, Miss Lyra.

Don't you chide me with not caring about the boy. I even care about you—though you've given me little enough reason and no thanks.

Good evening, Lyra. I'm glad you could come.

Master ...

... I've got to talk to you about something. It's very important.

Not right now, Lyra.

First of all, I'd like to introduce you to someone.

But—

Mrs. Coulter, this is our Lyra.

Lyra, say hello to Mrs. Coulter.

Good evening, Mrs. Coulter.

Hello, Lyra.

Oh, do you know my uncle?

That's true. I remember him telling me—

I met him at the Royal Arctic Institute. Last year I spent three months in Greenland observing the Aurora.

Are you an explorer too?

In a way. Would you like me to tell you about it?

So, Lyra. You've been talking to Mrs. Coulter. Did you enjoy hearing what she said?

Oh yes!

She's the most wonderful person I've ever met....

Quite.

Lyra, you've been safe here in Jordan College. I think you've been happy here. You've not found it easy to be obedient, but we're very fond of you and you've never been a bad child.

There's a great deal of goodness and sweetness in your nature. Lots of determination too. You'll need all of that.

There are things going on in the wide world that I'd have liked to protect you from, by keeping you here in Jordan.

But that's no longer possible.

NO!

No! I don't want to leave Jordan. I like it here. I want to stay here forever.

When you're young, you think that things last forever. Unfortunately, they don't. It won't be long before you become a young woman. You need female company.

I do not!

We're going to organize a cocktail party.

What for?

Because it'll be fun and your education has skipped over this sort of thing.

We'll buy you a new dress for the occasion, and you can help me with the invitation list. To start with, we absolutely must invite the Archbishop.

He's the most hateful old snob, but I can't afford to leave him out.

But I—

Lord Boreal is in town. And he's such fun.

And what about inviting the Princess Postnikova?

How pretty you look. I'm going to take you to the best hairdresser in London.

This way I'll have it with me all the time. It'll be safer.

What's the point? We won't be going to the North.

She's going to keep us here forever. When are we going to run away?

Why would she be teaching us navigation and all that, if she wasn't going to take us North?

To keep you quiet. You don't really want to stand around at the cocktail party being all sweet and pretty. She's making a pet out of you.

Why are you crying, Lyra?

I'm thinking about Roger.

But what makes me sad is that some days I don't even think about him at all.

So you're the famous Lyra?

A very fine reception your mother has organized.

Oh, she's not my mother!

My parents both died in an aeronautical accident in the North. They were a count and a countess.

Oh, really?

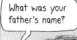

What was your father's name?

Count Belacqua. He was Lord Asriel's brother.

How interesting. And so what are you doing here, then?

I'm here to help. I'm Mrs. Coulter's personal assistant. I'll be accompanying her on her expeditions.

... Dust ...

... attracted by human beings ...

... by adults but not children ...

The General Oblation Board is entirely her own project.

But you, little lady...

... you don't need to be frightened of the General Oblation Board, do you?

Oh, I'm never scared. Not of gyptians who sell children like slaves to the Turks of the Bosphorus. Or of the werewolf at Godstow Priory ...

... not even of the Gobblers.

The Gobblers?

Yes, that's what the tabloids call the General Oblation Board. From the initials, you see.

Why "Oblation," though?

It's an old story. Back in the Middle Ages, parents gave their children to the Church to become monks or nuns. The unfortunate brats were known as "oblates," which means a sacrifice, an offering, something of that sort.

I see. Mrs. Coulter took up the idea again when she became interested in Dust.

More than an idea— it's a passion.

They say the children don't suffer, though.

Why don't you go and have a chat with Lord Boreal?

I'm sure he'd like to meet Mrs. Coulter's young protégée.

I'm hungry.

Can it be morning already?

Did you sleep well? Your cabin is lined with cedarwood.

It's supposed to have a soporific effect on dæmons.

Where are we?

Far away. It's important that you stay hidden. I don't want to see you up on deck.

They were Gobblers yesterday, weren't they?

Actually, we thought they'd taken you weeks ago.

Hey, have you ever heard of the Nälkäinens!

They're a kind of ghost they have up there. Same size as a child, but they've got no heads. They feel their way about at night, and if they get ahold of you, won't nothing make them let go.

And the Windsuckers, they're dangerous too. They drift about in the air. As soon as they touch you, all the strength goes out of you. You can't see 'em except as a kind of shimmer in the air.

And then there are the Breathless Ones, warriors half-killed. They wander about forever because the Tartars have snapped open their ribs and pulled out their lungs. They do it without killing them.

There's an art to it.

And then there's the panserbjørne. Hearda them?

Yes! My uncle is a prisoner in their fortress ... and the Gobblers are pleased, because they're not on his side.

The bears are like mercenaries. They sell their strength to whoever pays them. They're vicious killers, but they keep their word. When you make a bargain with an armored bear, you can rely on it.

Do they make their armor themselves?

Yes. They've got hands as deft as humans. They learned the trick of working with iron way back—meteoric iron mostly.

Are they allies of the Gobblers?

We're not sure. But what I do know is we're going to send a rescue party to free Billy and all the gyptian children.

What about my friend Roger? I have to rescue him. He'd have done the same for me.

The Gobblers are taking their prisoners to a town in the far North, way up in the land of dark.

What's certain is that they're doing it with the support of the police and the clergy. We can trust only ourselves.

What I'm proposing is dangerous. We must send a band of fighters to rescue the children and bring 'em back alive. If we're going to succeed, it will be at great cost to us.

There's landloper kids there too. Are we to rescue them as well?

Are you saying we should fight our way through every kind of danger just to rescue a small group of children and abandon the others? No, you're a better man than that....

Well, my friends, do I have your approval?

HURRAH!

HURRAH!

Aren't you, Chief Raymond?

Can you see any fish?

None.

Then I hope Ma Costa was joking when she said I'd only be eating ...

... what we bring back.

Hey!

You should pay more attention.

Many apologies, Lyra. I'm not as agile as I used to be.

I am Farder Coram, the oldest of the gyptians.

Ma Costa sent you here so that I could talk to you in private. Climb aboard my boat, please.

You won't know this, but I've been interested in your family for a long time. In fact, I know everything about you from the day you were born.

What could there be about me that's so interesting?

What do you know of your origins, Lyra?

Well ... my parents died in an airship accident. That's why Lord Asriel placed me in Jordan College.

Lies.

In truth, your father is ...

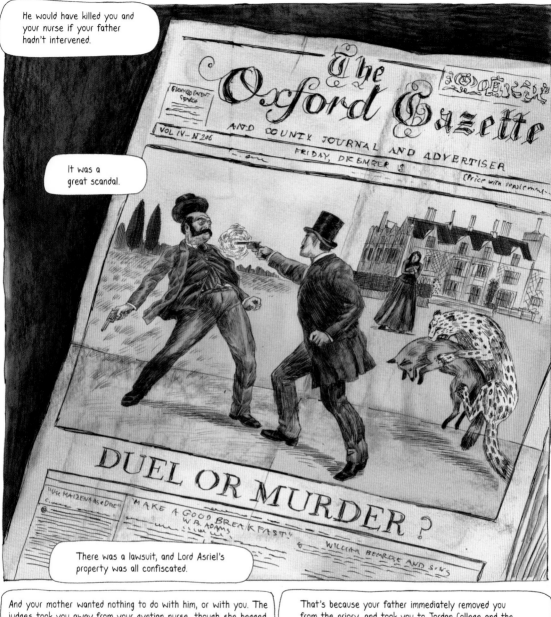

He would have killed you and your nurse if your father hadn't intervened.

It was a great scandal.

There was a lawsuit, and Lord Asriel's property was all confiscated.

And your mother wanted nothing to do with him, or with you. The judges took you away from your gyptian nurse, though she begged them not to, and placed you in the care of a priory.

I don't remember any of it.

That's because your father immediately removed you from the priory, and took you to Jordan College and the protection of the Master. The law courts didn't stop him.

Over here!

But then ... who's my mother?

The man Lord Asriel killed was called Edward Coulter.

Mrs. Coulter is my mother?!

That's awful!

She is your mother, and if your father weren't being held by the *panserbjørne*, she would never have dared defy him and you'd still be living at Jordan College.

What the Master was doing letting you go is a mystery I can't explain. He was charged with your care.

I believe the Master tried to keep his promise for as long as he could.

On the night I left, he gave me something. He said my uncle brought it to the College, and he made me promise never to show it to my mother.

I'm happy to show it to you, though.

OH!

The Master told me it was called an alethiometer.

A symbol reader! I never thought I'd set eyes on one again. Do you know how to use it?

I can make the three short hands move.

But I can't do anything with the long one. Except sometimes, if I concentrate very hard, I can make that hand go this way or that, just by thinking it.

Look. All these pictures around the rim are symbols. Take the anchor, there. Its first meaning is hope, for hope holds you fast like an anchor so you don't give way.

But it also means steadfastness, and prevention, as well as the sea, of course.... In fact, for each symbol there's a never-ending series of meanings!

Do you know them all?

I know some. There's a book that explains them all. I've seen it, and I know where it is, but—

JOHN FAA!

You humiliated me in front of my clan and all the gyptian people.

For that, I'm going to kill you!

Many people have tried, Chief Raymond.

Aaagh!

Thank you, clan chieftains.

We've a muster of 170 men. We have collected more gold than I expected. We can now charter a ship and sail north.

Na na na na na!

I don't know what you're playing at, little girl. But whatever it is, nothing's going to make me leave my post.

Huh?

Good evening.

I've brought you some cakes.

From what we know, there will be some fighting to do. Some of us will die, but we ain't coming back without our kids.

That child, Lord Faa. The police are searching our boats. There's a move in Parliament to rescind our ancient privileges to the waterways. Who is this child that we should come to such a pass?

This girl is the daughter of Lord Asriel. In case any of you have forgotten, he saved Sam Broekman when he was captured by the Turks.

PART II

BOLVANGAR

Do the Lapland witches live here at Trollesund, Farder Coram?

No, they live in forests and on the tundra. Their business is with the wild, but they keep a consul here.

Lord Faa told me you were friends with a witch.

Let's say there's an obligation there.

Lyra ...

I'm afraid to tell you this after what you done, but that little boy died an hour ago.

Lyra!

No one can survive without their dæmon.

Where's his fish?!

What does it matter?

Perhaps he ate it?

DON'T YOU DARE LAUGH. I'LL TEAR YOUR LUNGS OUT IF YOU LAUGH AT HIM.

It was all he had to cling onto. Who took it from him?

Easy, child.

I didn't know. I thought it was just what he'd been eating. I took it out of his hand because I thought it was more respectful. I gave it to my dogs.

Lend me your knife.

I hope that'll do, Tim, if I provide for you like a Jordan Scholar.

Lee...

Could you carry Iorek and his armor in your balloon?

I've done it before.

I rescued him one time from the Tartars—they had him trapped and were starving him out.

Bears aren't made to fly, but Lee saved me that day.

I've got a bad feeling about this.

Do you still have the alethiometer with you?

It's in my coat... and the spy-fly tin is in my boot.

Lost child. Bring to you.

Good work, Chief.

You speak English?

Yes.

Come in quickly.

We'll look after you here—don't worry.

ROAAAAAR

Who are you?

Medea. I'm a witch.

Pantalaimon!

Hey!

Perhaps the first witch you've met?

PART III

SVALBARD

But this ain't the job I signed up for. Now I'm risking my life and my equipment in a war. I need to know the risks.

It's too late to make choices now, Mr. Scoresby.

As soon as Lyra crossed your path, you stopped being a mercenary. You should now think of yourself as a recruit, under arms, a soldier.

I feel like a pawn in your game. Seems to me a man should have a choice whether to take up arms or not.

You're not just a pawn—you're a major player. We expect a lot from you.

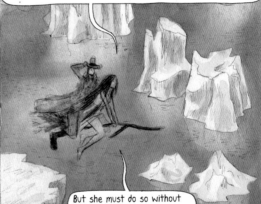

You see, Mr. Scoresby, there's a curious prophecy about this child: She is destined to bring about the end of destiny.

But she must do so without knowing what she is doing . . .

. . . as if it were her nature and not her destiny to do it. If she's told what she must do, all will fail; death will sweep through all the worlds, and despair will triumph, forever.

How far are we from Svalbard?

If we meet no winds, we shall be over Svalbard in twelve hours or so.

Where are we going to land?

It depends on the weather. We'll try to avoid the cliffs, though. There are foul creatures living there.

What's going to happen when I find Lord Asriel?

Lyra, be careful!

Should I tell him I know he's my father?

Will he want to come back to Oxford?

I don't think he will, Lyra.

It seems that there is something to be done in another world, and Lord Asriel is the only one who can bridge the gulf between that world and this.

But he needs something to help him.

The alethiometer!

How long do witches live, Serafina Pekkala?

Lyra, wake up! You're bewitched!

I am three hundred years or more. Our oldest witch mother is nearly a thousand. One day the goddess of the dead, Yambe-Akka, will come for her—smiling and kindly—when it's time to die.

Are there men witches?

No, men pass in front of our eyes like butterflies, creatures of a brief season. We love them; they are brave, proud, beautiful, clever.

But, alas, they die so soon that our hearts are continually racked with pain.

I loved Farder Coram. I stayed with him long enough to bear him a little boy, who died of a sickness that came out of the East. His death tore pieces out of my heart, and it broke Coram's.

Why did you leave him? You could have had more children.

Lyra, don't look down!

We've lit a fire for you, Lyra Silvertongue.

Come and sit with us, and hear what I am being told.

Speak now, Søren Eisarson.

Yes, er... um...

You must believe we never desired your exile, King Iorek. Mrs. Coulter is responsible. She has been manipulating Iofur for a long time—it was she who engineered your downfall.

She wanted to set up another station here like Bolvangar. Little by little she was increasing her power over Iofur—making us do unbearlike things.

What is she doing now, Lyra?

She's got a transport zeppelin...

... a zeppelin that's armed with machine guns, heading for Svalbard right now. She's waiting for reinforcements from a regiment of Tartars that's coming by sea.

She was pretending to help, but really she wants to overthrow Iofur, because he was helping Lord Asriel pursue his study of Dust.

She already knows we're here, from the cliff-ghasts, but she don't know yet that you've killed Iofur and taken power.

Oh! It's coming clear now: she wants to kill Lord Asriel. She knows what he's trying to do, and she fears it....

It must be the city in the sky! She's trying to get to it first.

And she wants something I've got, because she knows Lord Asriel needs it to achieve his aims. I think ... it must be the alethiometer.